Meet My Flowertot Friends

HarperCollins *Children's Books*

Hello!

My name is Fifi-Forget-Me-Not.

I live here,

in Flowertot Garden.

All my Flowertot friends

live here, too.

Would you like to meet them?

Come and meet Bumble.

Bumble is my best friend.

He lives in Honeysuckle House.

That's funny!

Bumble is not at home.

I wonder if he is at the

Flowertot Market?

This is the Flowertot Market.

And this is my friend, Poppy.

Poppy loves to chat
with her friends.
She sells lots of
yummy things to eat.
Bumble is not here!
Perhaps Violet has seen him.

This is Violet.
Violet is quite shy
but she is very kind.
She is also very good
at painting.

Violet lives in Flowertot Cottage

with her best friend,

Primrose.

Hello Primrose!
Primrose always
looks neat and tidy.
She hates mess.

Primrose can be
a bit bossy at times
but she is kind.
She likes to make
pretty things
for her friends.

Once Primrose painted
Bumble's door pink.
Bumble was not very pleased.
He likes his door to be red!

Where is Bumble?
Perhaps Stingo or
Slugsy knows
where he is.

Hello Stingo!
Stingo lives here,
in Apple Tree House.
He sees everything
that happens in the garden
through his telescope.

Hello Slugsy!

Slugsy is Stingo's best friend.

He lives here, in this den.

Stingo shouts when he
wants Slugsy's help.

We have to watch out
when Stingo and Slugsy
are around.

They get up to lots of tricks.

Slugsy loves Primrose.

He is always trying

to make her happy.

Everyone loves Aunt Tulip
and her pet, Grubby.
Aunt Tulip loves to chatter
with her Flowertot friends.

She has the best tea parties

and she always has

a funny story to tell.

But Bumble is not here.

Perhaps he is with Pip.

Pip likes to help
Bumble and me.
We have lots of fun
when Pip is around.

We have to keep
an eye on Pip.
Sometimes Stingo and Slugsy
get him to do silly things.

Buttercups and Daisies!
It's time to go home
and you still haven't met
my best friend, Bumble.
Where can he be?

Take me home, please, Mo!
Mo takes me
everywhere I need to go.
I don't know what
I would do without him!

Oh Bumble! There you are!

Where have you been?

A pot of honey! Yummy!

Thank you, Bumble!

Bumble is my very best friend.

He is such a happy little bee!

Which of my Flowertot

friends do you like best?

Created by Keith Chapman

First published in Great Britain in 2007 by HarperCollins Children's Books.
HarperCollins Children's Books is a division of HarperCollins Publishers Ltd.

1 3 5 7 9 10 8 6 4 2

ISBN-13: 978-0-00-732235-0

© Chapman Entertainment Ltd 2007
Visit Fifi at www.fifiandtheflowertots.com

Printed and bound in China